If You Take a Mouse to the Movies

A Special Christmas Edition

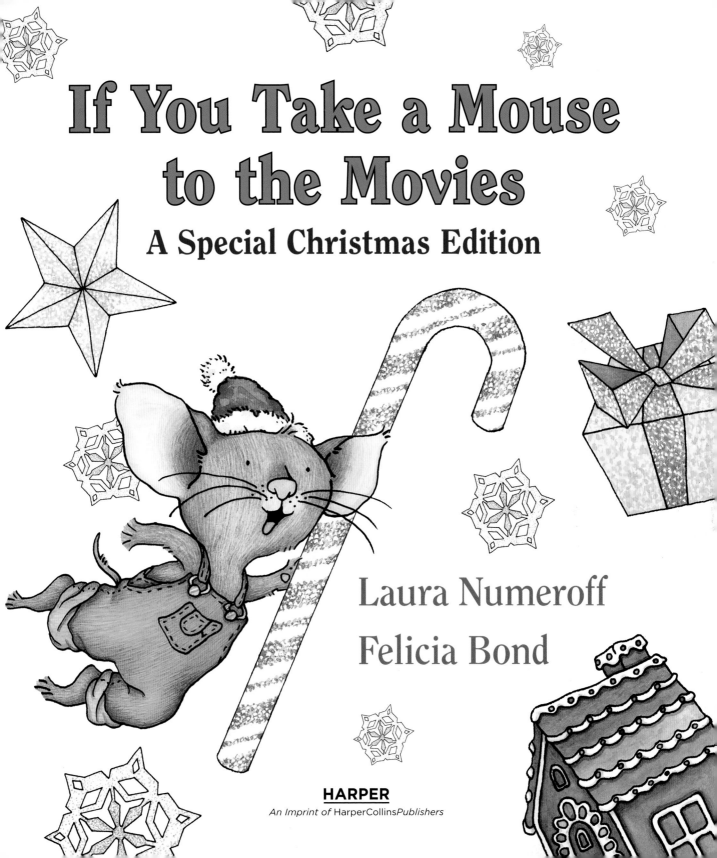

Laura Numeroff

Felicia Bond

HARPER

An Imprint of HarperCollinsPublishers

Visit www.mousecookiebooks.com

Library of Congress Catalog Card Number: 2009925577
ISBN 978-0-06-176280-2

Typography by Neil Swaab
09 10 11 12 13 SCP 10 9 8 7 6 5 4 3 2 1 ❖ First Edition

is a registered trademark of HarperCollins Publishers

When cooking, it is important to keep safety in mind. Children should always ask permission
from an adult before cooking and should be supervised by an adult in the kitchen at all times.
The publisher and authors disclaim any liability from any injury that might result from the use,
proper or improper, of the recipes and activities contained in this book.

Table of Contents

There were so many things I loved about the holidays as a little girl that I would run out of paper if I listed them all. One of my favorite memories is walking down Fifth Avenue in Manhattan to see the magic created in the department store windows. You actually have to wait in line but it is well worth it!

My dad would buy a small bag of warm chestnuts from a street vendor and we would share them as we tried to find the best store display. And we never skipped seeing the giant Christmas tree in Rockefeller Center. I could never figure out how they put so many lights on it.

When it got really cold out, my mother would warm my clothes in the oven before I put them on. Our driveway had a very small slope, but I never tired of going down it on my sled. One year, I made a snow bear! Afterward, hot chocolate with marshmallows was the perfect way to end the afternoon.

Now I live in Los Angeles, where it can be in the 80s during the holidays, so I like to go back home to New York. I walk down Fifth Avenue to look in the department store windows, visit the tree in Rockefeller Center, and munch on chestnuts. It brings back all the wonderful memories I have from the holidays!

Love,

Laura Numeroff

The holidays are such a special and exciting time for so many of us. There are tiny lights decorating houses and stores; there is music; there are treats and cookies and family dinners with favorite foods; and there is gift giving.

I have six brothers and sisters, and my parents always told us to remember people who had less than we did, so we'd all put some of our allowance in the sidewalk pots for the poor every Christmas. The Santa ringing the bell there would always say, "Thank you," and smile at us.

Some of the images in *If You Take a Mouse to the Movies* were inspired by things my brothers and sisters and I did as children. But my favorite picture in the book was something I made up completely. It's the one in the beginning, when Mouse gets to ride in the boy's hood. I imagined how good that would feel, to both Mouse and the boy.

I had many favorite books that my mother brought out every year in December. One was very tiny, with a cat, a rabbit, a dog, and a little girl. Many, many years later I made a book that was also tiny in size. It was the second book I ever made and is still special to me.

Reading books is a way of connecting with something inside of us and also with other people. Mouse has a lot of imagination and makes us laugh, too. I think he's super cool.

Love,

Felicia Bond

IF YOU TAKE A MOUSE TO THE MOVIES

BY **Laura Numeroff**

ILLUSTRATED BY **Felicia Bond**

For my wonderful mom,
Florence Numeroff

—*L.N.*

For Laura Geringer

—*F.B.*

If You Take a Mouse to the Movies

If You Take a

BY Laura Numeroff

ILLUSTRATED BY Felicia Bond

A Laura Geringer Book

An Imprint of HarperCollins*Publishers*

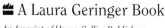

Mouse to the Movies

If You Take a Mouse to the Movies
Text copyright © 2000 by Laura Numeroff
Illustrations copyright © 2000 by Felicia Bond
All rights reserved.
www.harpercollinschildrens.com
Library of Congress Cataloging-in-Publication Data
Numeroff, Laura Joffe.
If you take a mouse to the movies / by Laura
Numeroff ; illustrated by Felicia Bond.
    p.   cm.
Summary: Taking a mouse to the movies can
    lead to letting him do other things, such as
    making a snowman, listening to Christmas
    carols, and decorating the Christmas tree.
ISBN 978-0-06-027868-7 (lib. bdg.) ISBN 978-0-06-027867-0
[1. Mice—Fiction. 2. Christmas—Fiction.]
    I. Bond, Felicia, ill. II. Title.
PZ7.N964Ij 2000   99-27258
[E]—DC21   CIP
                                              AC

NOW SHOWING

AN IF YOU
GIVE... BOOK™

is a registered trademark of HarperCollins Publishers

If you take a mouse to the movies,

he'll ask you for some popcorn.

When you give him the popcorn,

he'll want to string it all together.

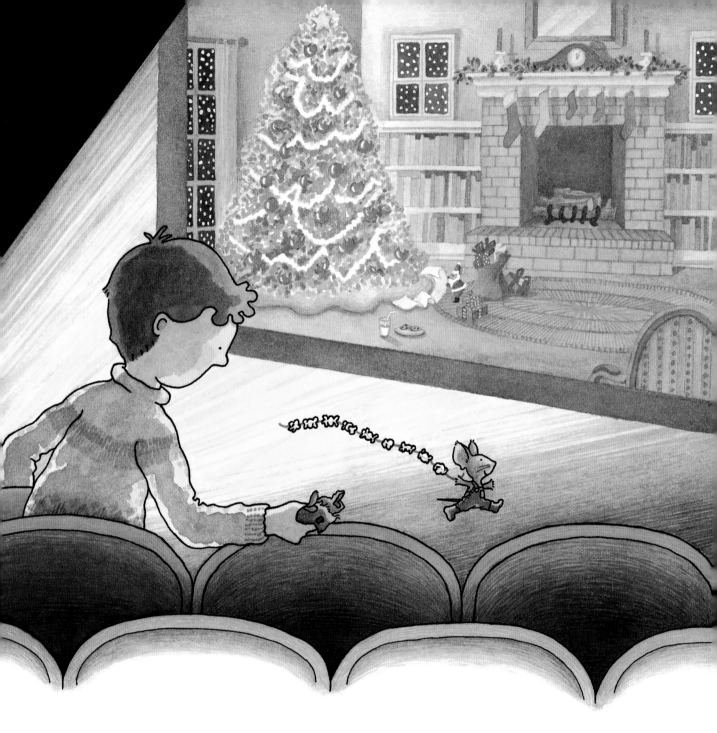

Then he'll want to hang it on a Christmas tree.

You'll have to buy him one.

On the way home, he'll see a
snowman in your neighbor's yard.
He'll want to make one of his own.

Then he'll need a carrot for a nose.

When he's all finished, he'll decide to build a fort.
He'll ask you to help him.

Then he'll want to make
some snowballs and have
a snowball fight.

Playing outside will make him cold.
He'll want to go inside and curl up on the couch.

He'll ask you for a blanket.

Once he's nice and cozy,
he'll want to listen to Christmas carols.

You'll have to find some on the radio.

He'll probably sing along.

The carols will remind him of his Christmas tree,
so he'll want to make ornaments.

You'll get him some paper and glue.

He'll ask you for glitter.

When the ornaments are done,

he'll hang them all up.

Then he'll stand back
to look at the tree.

He'll notice his popcorn string is missing!

So he'll want to make another one.

He'll ask you for some popcorn.

And chances are,
when you give him the popcorn,

he'll want you to take him to the movies.

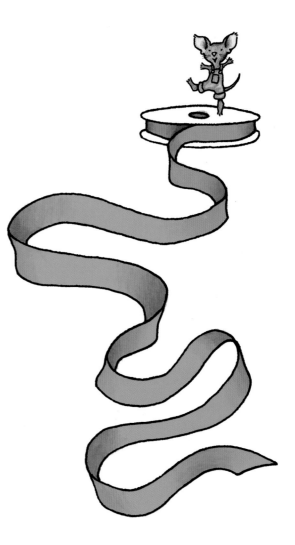

What Can You Find on Mouse's Christmas Tree?

One of Mouse's favorite things about Christmas is getting to decorate his tree. He uses tons and tons of ornaments. Can you find his gingerbread cookie ornament shaped like a snowman? How about the mouse nutcracker ornament? Can you find all six elf ornaments? How about all sixteen wrapped present ornaments? And can you find Mouse, hiding in his tree, wearing red overalls?

How to Make Your Own Elf Ornaments, Just Like Mouse!

What you need to get started:

Paper

Scissors

Markers, crayons, colored pencils,
   or paint

White liquid glue

Paintbrush

Glitter

Yarn

 1. Trace the elf outline onto a new piece of paper with your markers or crayons.

2. Fill in your elf with color! You can use paint, markers, crayons, or even colored pencils. (When Felicia Bond made her elf ornaments, she used watercolors.)

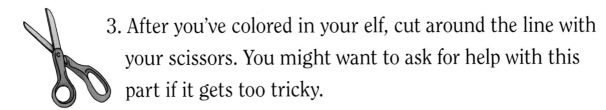

3. After you've colored in your elf, cut around the line with your scissors. You might want to ask for help with this part if it gets too tricky.

4. Now it's time to add glitter! First paint some white liquid glue on your elf's hat and suit. Then shake your favorite glitter colors onto your elf and put him aside to dry.

5. After the glue is all dry, shake him off over a trash bin so you don't make a mess with the extra glitter.

6. Now it's time to poke a hole with the pencil in your elf's hat, where the dot is in the tracing. Pick your favorite color yarn to thread through your elf, cut a two-inch piece, poke it through the hole, and then tie the two ends in a double knot.

7. Your elf is ready to be hung on a tree!

8. Since Santa has many elf helpers, you can make as many elves as you want and color each one differently.

SANTA'S mouse's ^FAVORITE
CHOCOLATE CHIP COOKIES

18 cookies • 350°F oven

1 cup plus 2 tablespoons flour
½ teaspoon baking soda
pinch salt
½ cup softened butter
1 teaspoon vanilla extract
½ cup sugar

¼ cup packed light brown sugar
1 egg
1 cup red and green little candy-coated chocolates

1. Combine the flour, baking soda, and salt. Set aside.
2. In a bowl, mash together the butter, vanilla, sugar, and brown sugar until smooth and fluffy. Add the egg. Gradually add the flour mixture and mix until just blended. Stir in the chocolates, adding 1 teaspoon of water if necessary to help mix.
3. Drop batter by tablespoon onto greased cookie sheets. Bake for 10–12 minutes.

FELICIA BOND'S
CHOCOLATE REFRIGERATOR ROLL

Makes 12 servings

1 teaspoon vanilla extract
2 cups heavy cream, whipped
1 9-oz. container of chocolate wafer cookies
4 large candy canes

1. Stir vanilla into whipped cream.
2. Set out wafer cookies.
3. Spread half a tablespoon of whipped cream onto each wafer.
4. Make stacks of wafers and whipped cream, then stand them on edge on a serving platter to make a 14-inch log.
5. Frost with remaining whipped cream.
6. Put candy canes in a tightly sealed sandwich bag and crush with a rolling pin. Sprinkle on top of log.
7. Chill for 4–6 hours.
8. To serve, slice at 45-degree angle.

Felicia says: As children, my brother and sisters and I loved making this because we would eat all the broken wafers in the package and lick the whipped cream off the eggbeater. Yum!

LAURA NUMEROFF'S FAVORITE
NORWEGIAN CHRISTMAS COOKIES

48 cookies • 350°F oven

2 large eggs
1 cup sugar
4 cups flour
1 teaspoon baking powder
3 sticks salted butter, softened
½ cup sugar cubes (coarsely crushed)

1. Beat together one egg and sugar with an electric mixer until thick and pale.
2. Sift in flour and baking powder.
3. Add butter. Beat on low speed until mixture forms a dough.
4. Chill, wrapped in plastic wrap, until firm, at least 1 hour.
5. While dough is chilling, put sugar cubes in a sandwich bag, seal shut, and crush with a rolling pin.
6. Lightly beat remaining egg.
7. Roll tablespoons of dough into balls and arrange one inch apart on ungreased baking sheets.
8. Press your thumb into center of each ball to flatten, leaving a print, and brush lightly with egg.
9. Sprinkle crushed sugar in centers and bake in batches in middle of oven until golden brown, 12–18 minutes. Transfer to racks to cool completely.

51

Mouse's Favorite

Singing Christmas Carols

Making Ornaments   Red Overalls

Christmas Trees   Popcorn Garlands

Baking Cookies   Smelling Cookies

Snuggling in Blankets   Candy Cane Shorts

Tasting Cookies   Building Snowmice

Making Snow Forts   Having Snowball Fights

Drinking Hot Chocolate

Going to the Movies

Candy Canes

What do you love about Christmas and winter?
You can make your own list, just like Mouse!

Christmas Things

Getting Presents

The Poem with "Not a creature was stirring, not even a mouse"

Winter Hats   Sparkling Lights   Eating Cookies

Swallowing Cookies   Gingerbread Houses

Wrapping Paper   Waiting Up for Santa   Ice-Skating

Spending Time with Family   Giving Cookies to Friends

Playing with New Toys   Chewing Cookies

Mittens   Ribbons

Candles   Having Friends Over

Write Your Own Christmas Story!

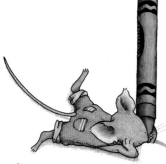

In *If You Take a Mouse to the Movies*, Mouse does lots of things to get ready for Christmas. You can write a story about what you do to get ready for Christmas, too. Here's a fill-in-the-blanks guide for you. Be sure to draw pictures to go along with your story!

 Page 1: I celebrate Christmas with _____, _____, _____, and _____.

Page 2: ____ days before Christmas, we decorate our tree. My favorite ornament is _____.

Page 3: Our tree always has a(n) _____ on the tip-top. This year, _____ put it up there.

 Page 4: We also make special food for Christmas. _____ cooks Christmas dinner. My favorite part is the _____. It's delicious!

Page 5: On Christmas Eve, we always _____ _____.

 Page 6: Then, on Christmas morning, we _____ _____.

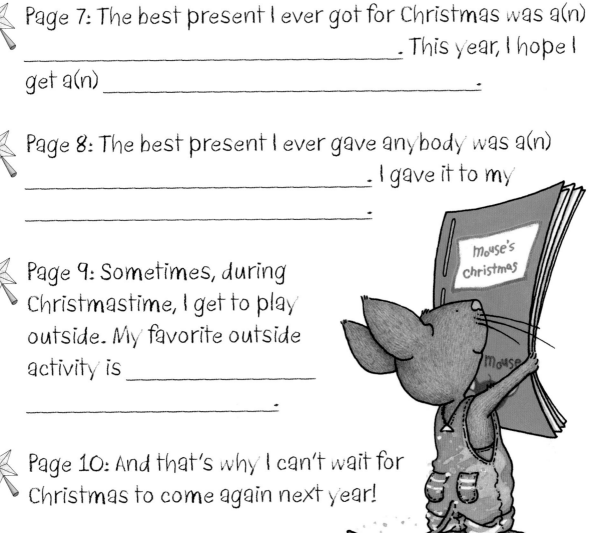 Page 7: The best present I ever got for Christmas was a(n) _____. This year, I hope I get a(n) _____.

Page 8: The best present I ever gave anybody was a(n) _____. I gave it to my _____.

Page 9: Sometimes, during Christmastime, I get to play outside. My favorite outside activity is _____ _____.

Page 10: And that's why I can't wait for Christmas to come again next year!

Real-Life Stories About the Holidays from Laura Numeroff and Felicia Bond

I used to help my best friend, Pat, decorate her tree. I always put on way too much tinsel! —LN

My favorite things at Christmas are the lights! I wish they would keep them up all year long! —LN

I've always liked to cook. When I was seven my mother started to teach me how. At Christmas I would make little pastries out of pie dough, butter, sugar, and cinnamon. I think the most I ever ate at once was fifteen. I still make these pastries today. —FB

I love trying food from different countries. One Christmas, my friend and I found a recipe for Norwegian Christmas cookies in a cookbook. They've now become my favorite treat for the holidays! They make great gifts, too! —LN

I have four brothers and two sisters. We would all get gifts for each other to put under the tree. I used to make my own wrapping paper with felt-tip pens. —FB

At Christmas I used to creep downstairs at night when everyone was asleep and stare at the Christmas tree. My favorite ornaments were an angel with a blue foil gown and hair of gold silk, and a tiny wood soldier who was painted bright colors. He was playing a drum. That's where I got the idea to make a drawing of Mouse with his drum in this book. —FB

57

Mouse's 12 Days of Christmas

by Sarah Weeks

On the first day of Christ-mas my mouse__ gave to me a great big__ choc'-late chip cook-ie.__ On the sec-ond day of Christ-mas my mouse__ gave to me two bend-y straws and a great big__ choc'-late chip cook-ie.__ On the third day of Christ-mas my mouse__ gave to me three sips of milk, two bend-y straws, and a great big__ choc'-late chip cook-ie.__ On the fourth day of Christ-mas my mouse__ gave to me

four pop-corn strings, three sips of milk, two bend-y straws, and a

great big_ choc'-late chip cook-ie.___ On the fifth day of Christ-mas my

mouse_ gave to me five pairs of box-er shorts (green with can-dy canes),

four_ pop-corn strings, three sips of milk, two_ bend-y straws, and a

great big_ choc'-late chip cook-ie.___ On the sixth day of Christ-mas my

mouse_ gave to me six per-fect pine trees, five pairs of box-er

shorts (green with can-dy canes), four_ pop-corn strings, three sips of milk,

59

two — ben-dy straws, and a great big — choc'-late chip cook-ie.___ On the

sev-enth day of Christ-mas my mouse — gave to me sev-en snow-balls fly-ing,

six per-fect pine trees, five pairs of box-er shorts (green with can-dy canes),

four — pop-corn strings, three sips of milk, two — ben-dy straws, and a

great big — choc'-late chip cook-ie.___ On the eighth day of Christ-mas my

mouse gave to me eight snow-men melt-ing, sev-en snow-balls fly-ing,

six per-fect pine trees, five pairs of box-er shorts (green with can-dy canes),

60

four — pop-corn strings, three sips of milk, two — bend-y straws, and a

great big — choc'-late chip cook-ie.— On the ninth day of Christ-mas my

mouse — gave to me nine co-zy blank-ets, eight snow-men melt-ing,

sev-en snow-balls fly-ing, six per-fect pine trees, five pairs of box-er

shorts (green with can-dy canes), four — pop-corn strings, three sips of milk,

two — bend-y straws, and a great big — choc'-late chip cook-ie.— On the

tenth day of Christ-mas my mouse — gave to me ten ra-dios blar-ing,

61

nine co-zy blank-ets, eight snow-men melt-ing, sev-en snow-balls fly-ing,

six per-fect pine trees, five pairs of box-er shorts (green with can-dy canes),

four __ pop-corn strings, three sips of milk, two __ bend-y straws, and a

great big __ choc'-late chip cook-ie.__ On the e-lev-enth day of Christ-mas my

mouse __ gave to me e-lev-en or-na-ments glit-ter-ing, ten ra-dios blar-ing,

nine co-zy blank-ets, eight snow-men melt-ing, sev-en snow-balls fly-ing,

six per-fect pine trees, five pairs of box-er shorts (green with can-dy canes),

A Christmas Medley: Mouse-Style

by Sarah Weeks

O Christ-mas tree, O Christ-mas tree, I like the way you look there. Each or-na-ment and can-dy cane how neat-ly on its hook there. Some mice might choose to trim their trees with lit-tle chunks of ched-dar cheese, but Christ-mas tree, O Christ-mas tree, we're trim-ming you with strings of pop-corn, pop pop pop pop pop pop pop pop pop! From the bot-tom

pop pop pop pop pop pop pop pop pop pop pop pop

pop pop pop pop sound! Pop-corn on a piece of string

is a ve-ry love-ly thing. Luh _____

___ luh _____ luh _____ love - ly thing.

Pop-corn on a string is luh _____ luh _____

luh _____ a love - ly thing! Hey, ev' - ry -

one, I think we're done. No ker - nels left to

string._____ Now that we're fin - ished with the tree, come
down for a mer - ry dance with me. Come dance and sing with___
me! Come___ dance and sing with___ me! Come___
dance___ and sing_____ a - round the tree!
We've all sung a mer - ry med - ley, we've
all sung a mer - ry med - ley, we've all sung a mer - ry med - ley._____
___ Now let's take a lit - tle nap!

DRUM

top & bottom: measure cylinder.

fold all five little circles and glue to drums cylinder last.

roll to make cylinder and glue ends

but color and glitter first,

Then thread yarn or string across 2 sides to han...

mitten

CANDLE ORNAMENT

crumple foil to look like a flame

tin foil flame

1½" flame

3" candle

1" base

4" roll into tight cylinder

Colored paper

FOLD ALONG RED LINES

base

glue

glue

A

cut hole for bottom of candle to go into

mash at bottom to fit into top of candle

cut hole & glue to A

lights from tree will make foil flame "flicker"

...and one
more, just
for fun.

The End